Animobiles

Animals on the MOOove

words and pictures by
Maddie Frost

sourcebooks
jabberwocky

Published by Jabberwocky, an imprint of Sourcebooks, Inc.
P.O. Box 4410, Naperville, Illinois 60567-4410
(630) 961-3900
Fax: (630) 961-2168
sourcebooks.com

Library of Congress Cataloging-in-Publication Data

Names: Frost, Maddie, author.
Title: Animobiles: animals on the mooove / Maddie Frost.
Description: Naperville, Illinois : Sourcebooks Jabberwocky, [2018] |
    Summary: Illustrations and simple, rhyming text reveal what happens when
    vehicles and animals are combined into such things as a tiger-train,
    parrot-plane, or salmon-submarine.
Identifiers: LCCN 2017008284 | (13 : alk. paper)
Subjects: | CYAC: Stories in rhyme. | Vehicles--Fiction. | Animals--Fiction.
    | Imaginary creatures--Fiction.
Classification: LCC PZ8.3.F934 Vro 2018 | DDC [E]--dc23 LC record available at https://lccn.loc.
gov/2017008284

Source of Production: Leo Paper, Heshan City, Guangdong Province, China
Date of Production: February 2018
Run Number: 5011242

Printed and bound in China.
LEO 10 9 8 7 6 5 4 3 2 1

FOR ALLi

Some vehicles go **VROOM!**

Some animals say **ROAR!**

Put them both together
and find out what's in store!

Racing over grassy fields,
  a **TIGER-TRAIN** is on a track.
Families look out their windows
  as the wheels go clickety-clack.

Under swooping jungle vines
MONKEY-MOPEDS zoom with glee.
One shouts out, "Let's race!
I bet you can't catch me!"

Above the giant treetops
PARROT-PLANES zigzag and glide.

Time to boost the engine
and snatch fruit along the ride!

On shores of sunny beaches
TRACTOR-TURTLES tread on sand.

They're digging out safe places
for the hatchlings up on land.

Down beneath the river
swims a **SALMON-SUBMARINE**.
It glides against the current
as it travels up the stream.

On the open country roads
COW-CARS MOOOve in any weather.

They stop and go for grass
and always stick together.

Cruising through the seas,
SEAL-SHIPS float in perfect file.

Finding spots to drop their anchors
to go fishing for a while.

The garden grooves to the beat
as **BEE-BLIMPS** buzz for hours.

Their landing gear is ready—
time to rest upon the flowers.

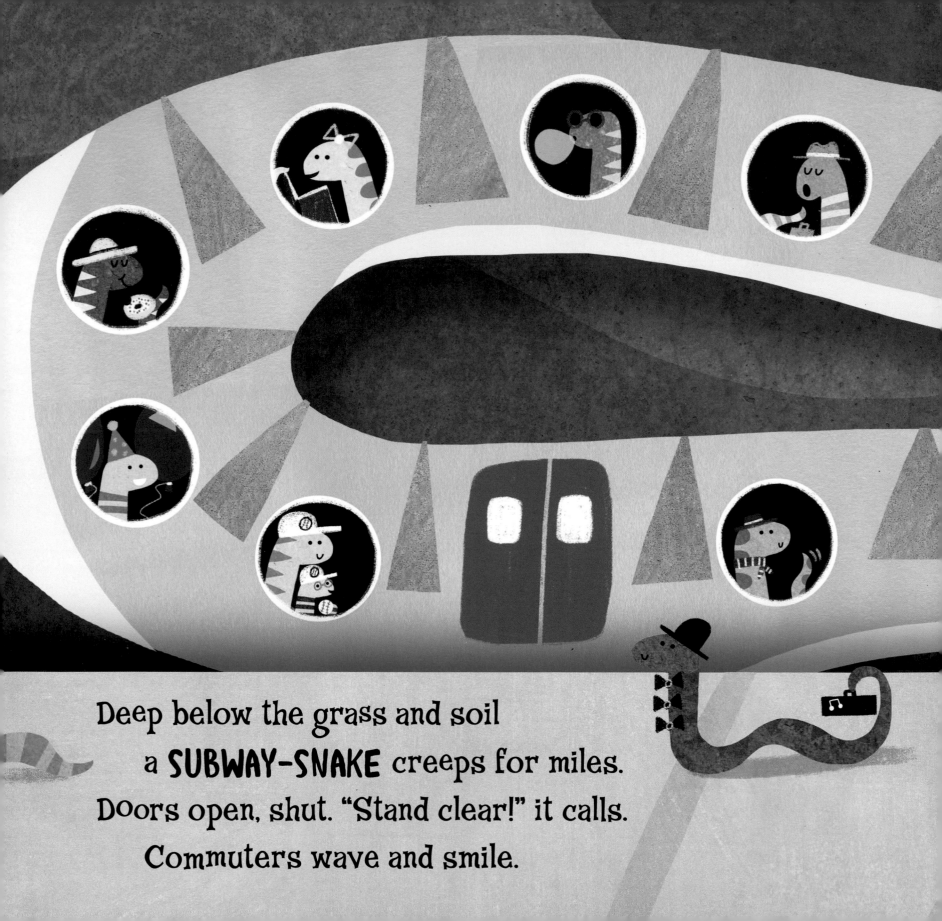

Deep below the grass and soil
a **SUBWAY-SNAKE** creeps for miles.
Doors open, shut. "Stand clear!" it calls.
Commuters wave and smile.

Inside the quiet forest
  a **BEAR-BUS** carries tired friends.
They get ready with a YAWWWN
  to fall asleep back in their dens.

Way up in the starry sky
BAT-BALLOONS float through the night.
They help each other navigate
while enjoying moonlit flight.

These passengers had so much fun—
in water, land, and sky.

But the animals **ARE ON THE GO...**

So HONK

and say "Goodbye!"